Haruki Murakami: Best-Selling Author

✳ Influential Asians ✳

HARUKI MURAKAMI

Best-Selling Author

John A. Torres

Enslow Publishing
101 W. 23rd Street
Suite 240
New York, NY 10011
USA
enslow.com

Published in 2017 by Enslow Publishing, LLC.
101 W. 23rd Street, Suite 240, New York, NY 10011

Copyright © 2017 by Enslow Publishing, LLC.

All rights reserved.

No part of this book may be reproduced by any means without the written permission of the publisher.

Library of Congress Cataloging-in-Publication Data

Names: Torres, John Albert, author.
Title: Haruki Murakami : best-selling author / John A. Torres.
Description: New York, NY : Enslow Publishing, 2017. | Series: Influential Asians | Includes bibliographical references and index.
Identifiers: LCCN 2015046324 | ISBN 9780766079014 (library bound)
Subjects: LCSH: Murakami, Haruki, 1949—Juvenile literature. | Authors, Japanese—20th century—Biography—Juvenile literature.
Classification: LCC PL856.U673 Z8925 2016 | DDC 895.63/5—dc23
LC record available at http://lccn.loc.gov/2015046324

Printed in the United States of America

To Our Readers: We have done our best to make sure all websites in this book were active and appropriate when we went to press. However, the author and the publisher have no control over and assume no liability for the material available on those websites or on any websites they may link to. Any comments or suggestions can be sent by e-mail to customerservice@enslow.com.

Photo Credits: Cover, pp. 3, 6 JOHN MACDOUGALL/AFP/Getty Images; p. 9 Junji Kurokawa/AFP/Getty Images; p. 11 STR/AFP/Getty Images; p. 16 Toru Yamakaka; p. 19 Kazuhiro Nogi/AFP/Getty Images; p. 23 Bernard Hoffman/The LIFE Picture Collection/Getty Images; p. 26 DEA / A. DAGLI ORTI/De Agostini/Getty Images; p. 27 Keystone/Hulton Archive/Getty Images; p. 31 JTB Photo/Universal Images Group/Getty Images; p. 34 Isaac Mok/Shutterstock.com; pp. 38, 69 © AP Images; p. 42 Ralph Crane/The LIFE Images Collection/Getty Images; p. 46 Hulton Archive/Hulton Archive/Getty Images; p. 49 Express Newspapers/Archive Photos/Getty Images; p. 52 Jeremy Sutton-Hibbert/Getty Images Entertainment; p. 56 Michael Cizek/AFP/Getty Images; pp. 64, 88, 103 YOSHIKAZU TSUNO/AFP/Getty Images; p. 67 Jeremy Sutton-Hibbert/Getty Images Entertainment; p. 72 Earl Theisen Collection/Archive Photos/Getty Images; p. 77 Rex Features/AP Photo; p. 81 Ulf Andersen/Hulton Archive/Getty Images; p. 85 John Lamparski/WireImage/Getty Images; p. 90 David Madison/Getty Images Sport; p. 94 TORU YAMANAKA/AFP/Getty Images; p. 99 XINHUA/Gamma-Rapho/Getty Images; pp. 109, 111 ullstein bild/Getty Images; p. 114 Jeremy Sutton-Hibbert/ Getty Images Entertainment.

Contents

1 **Only One of Six** 7

2 **Destiny** 17

3 **Rebelling** 29

4 **Western Influence** 40

5 **Finding His Way** 51

6 **Baseball** 61

7 **Best-Selling Author** 73

8 **Running to Commercial Success** 83

9 **Japan's 9/11** 95

10 **A Future Nobel Prize?** 105

Chronology 116

Chapter Notes 118

Glossary 123

Further Reading 124

Index 125

Haruki Murakami's writing is celebrated around the globe.

Chapter 1

ONLY ONE OF SIX

The news was terrible.

Someone or some group had spread poisonous gas throughout the Tokyo subway. No one knew what was going on, except that people were dying. Those who survived were getting terribly sick. Others were going blind.

The sarin gas attacks of March 20, 1995 would go down in history as the worst attack in Japan since the United States dropped two atom bombs on the island nation to end World War II.

Chaos

When the smoke finally cleared, twelve people were dead, fifty more were severely injured, and more than a thousand innocent passengers riding the train that morning experienced blindness or vision problems. In

World War II Atom Bombs

In one of the most controversial and deadly decisions of any war, the United States dropped two atomic bombs on Japan, which ultimately forced the Japanese to surrender and bring about the end of the war.

It was August 1945 and Germany—Japan's ally against the United States and Britain—had already surrendered. The United States asked the Japanese to surrender or they would face "total destruction."

The Japanese refused and on August 6, an American plane dropped an atomic bomb on Hiroshima, destroying the city and killing thousands. The Japanese still did not surrender.

On August 9, the United States dropped a second atomic bomb—this time on Nagasaki. The results were horrific. More than 130,000 Japanese citizens were killed and countless others crippled and exposed to radiation. Six days after the bomb leveled the city of Nagasaki, Japan surrendered and the war ended.

To this day, the United States remains the only country to ever use nuclear weapons against another country. The decision to drop the bombs remains a source of debate and controversy.

American military leaders estimated that invading Japan would result in more than 100,000 dead American soldiers, while dropping the bomb would end the war quickly and keep American soldiers alive. In the end, those supporting the bomb won out.

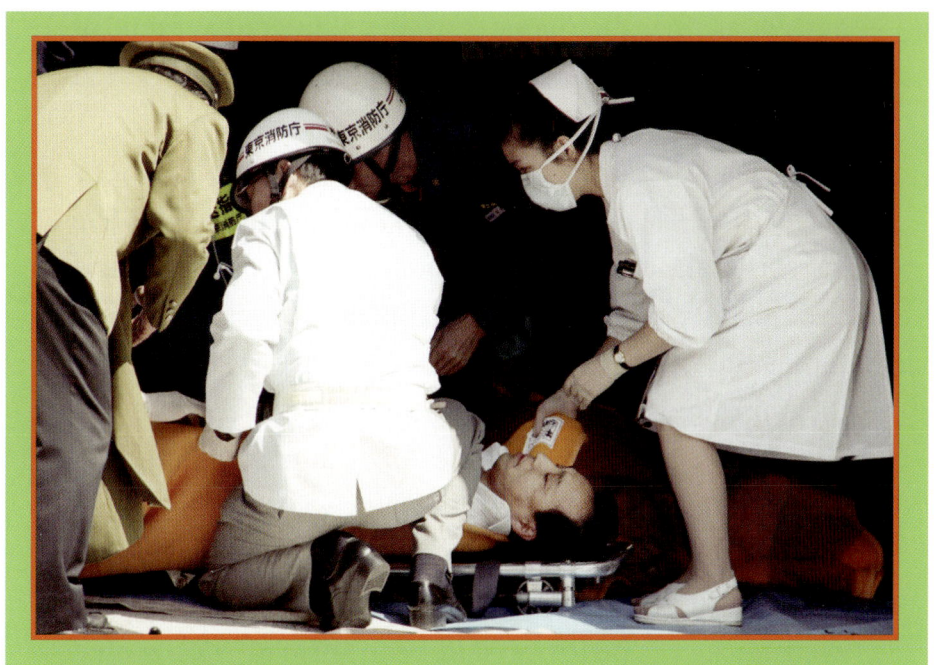

Emergency medical teams treat victims exposed to sarin gas fumes in the Tokyo subway system on March 20, 1995 during the Aum Shinrikyo attack.

total, more than five thousand survivors were treated at area hospitals that day.

The city was thrown into chaos as no one could know if there was more poison gas being released or how many more would die. There was uncertainty everywhere in a country that relied on routine and discipline, where everyone knew what their daily role was supposed to be.

Religious radicals who were part of an organization called Aum Shinrikyo were responsible for the terror. The group, known as a "doomsday cult," was trying to bring about the end of the world. They chose one of the busiest commuter railways in the world to carry out their attack during the hectic morning rush hour. In particular, five members carried a liquefied version of sarin, onto five different trains in plastic bags hidden in rolled-up newspapers.

That particular poisonous gas is so dangerous that a single drop is all that is needed to kill an adult. The five terrorists placed the bags of poison on the ground and then poked holes in them with the tips of their umbrellas. As the liquid began to evaporate, passengers breathed in the poisonous vapors, making them extremely sick.

This was not the first time Aum Shinrikyo had been involved in criminal activities. They were already being watched by the government for keeping cult members against their will, practicing extortion, kidnapping, and even murder. The group had been formally designated as a terrorist organization by several countries, including the United States.

Writing Underground

During the days, weeks, and months that followed, newspaper reports and television news programs focused on the terrorist group and their radical thinking. There was barely anything written about the victims, the ones who died and the ones who survived.

That is why the country's most famous author, Haruki Murakami, decided to take a break from writing his fantastical fiction stories to do something completely different. He decided to write a nonfiction piece, focusing all of his efforts on those who suffered, those whose lives had been changed forever. He did not like how the media seemed to sensationalize the attacks and

Only One of Six

Aum Shinrikyo's leader, Shoko Asahara, was convicted on several counts of murder in what was called the Trail of the Century in Japan.

how quickly the country wanted to move forward as if the attack had never happened.

What followed was a masterpiece of a book called *Underground*.

And Murakami could not go anywhere without being asked why he decided to write about the attacks.

"Everyone asks me that question, but I can't answer it very well," he said. "My most honest answer is that I felt I should do it. I wanted to listen to as many stories and in as much detail as possible from the people who were riding the subway that morning."[1]

Murakami interviewed sixty-five of the victims over the course of a year to try and write the most accurate account of the deadly attacks that he could.

What made the book so interesting for readers is that Murakami wrote the piece as a novel or story and focused on what the victims felt happened to them rather than just writing about the facts. "In that sense, although this is a form of non-fiction work, it is much more a novelist's work, without a doubt," he said.[2]

One of the toughest challenges Murakami faced when researching and then writing the book was having to deal with the culture and deep-seated traditions of his fellow countrymen and women. In fact, even though he interviewed more than sixty survivors, Murakami was not surprised that many survivors refused his request to be interviewed.

A Country's Mood

He was also fascinated by the country's attitude. He felt as if the Japanese people would rather ignore that an attack even took place in order to get on with their everyday lives.

What stunned Murakami as well was the slow and indecisive reaction of the country's emergency services, many of whom seemed not to know how to react to or treat the afflicted.

"In Japanese society, it is thought that those who suffer unfortunate deaths should be left in peace," he said. "If a similar thing had occurred in the U.S., I imagine a lot more information would have been made public."[3]

A strategy used by Murakami during the interview process and then while writing the book proved to be a stroke of genius that would set this book apart from anything else written about the tragedy.

Instead of solely focusing the book on what went on during the commuter train attacks, he went deeper. He asked about everyone's background, where they were going, and what their lives were like. He wanted to give each one of the victims he interviewed their own unique voice and their own unique story. This was not easy to do since, in Murakami's own words, in Japan "it is difficult to be an individual."[4]

Blind Nightmare

One of the most interesting and unique themes of the book had to do with how people dealt with what was

Sarin

Sarin is a colorless, odorless liquid that has been used as a type of nerve gas and is considered a weapon of mass destruction. When it evaporates, the sarin vapors are as deadly as the liquid form. The chemical was invented by Germany in the 1930s as a pesticide used to kill insects.

After sarin is released into the air, people can become exposed through skin contact or by breathing in the deadly vapors. It is especially deadly when used as a vapor, making people deathly sick within only a few seconds of being exposed. After being exposed to sarin, the body loses control of some bodily functions such as muscle movement and gland production. It causes blurry vision, blindness, runny nose, dizziness, nausea, and confusion. Eventually the body becomes tired, causing the exposed individual to stop breathing altogether. Someone exposed to sarin should immediately try to get to fresh air or into a shower where they should wash with a lot of soap and water.

In addition to the sarin attacks on the Tokyo subway, the Syrian government was in recent years accused to using sarin against rebel soldiers looking to overthrow the president. The deadly attack was condemned by the international community. The gas was reported to have killed more than 1,000 Syrians. The country of Iraq has also been accused of using sarin as a weapon of war.

happening to them that morning. As people were falling unconscious and others getting sick, no one spoke, yelled, screamed, or asked one another what was happening to them. There were even instances of people doing nothing at all to help those who had fallen to the ground, overcome by the gas. They simply ignored them until official help had arrived.

It was that kind of attitude that prompted Japan's most well-known author to finish the book with a personal essay called "Blind Nightmare: Where Are We Japanese Going?" The essay criticized the Japanese response to the attack and their willingness to move on so quickly instead of working to figure out why the attack occurred and how to prevent similar future incidents.

Those thoughts and themes that regularly make their way into Murakami's books are what generally sets him apart from other Japanese writers. His work is so different and so unique that it can be difficult to categorize. He is as popular in other countries—especially the United State—as he is in Japan.

But his renegade style also makes him a target for other writers and even critics. For example, even though his telling of the terror attack included interviews with the religious fanatics responsible, he was accused of being too one-sided.

That didn't bother him at all.

"Even now I can remember all of the victims' faces and voices, and yet I cannot remember those of the Aum people."[5]

Haruki Murakami: Best-Selling Author

In his writing, Murakami focused less on the members of Aum Shinrikyo and more on the victims of the sarin attack.

What will be remembered are the beautiful words this gentle, thoughtful Japanese writer has brought to the world over the years. And his life could easily have been ripped from the pages of one of his surreal novels. His is a tale of a young man who never thought he was good enough to write for a living but who would, of course, become one of the most influential and successful writers of our time.

Chapter 2

DESTINY

Haruki Murakami seemed destined to become a great writer even before his parents ever met. His father, Chiaki, and his mother Mikuyi, were raised during the glory years of the Japanese empire but then also lived through some of the country's darkest hours.

Japan joined with the allies—United States and Britain—near the end of World War I and seized several important parcels of land that had previously been in dispute. This emboldened the Japanese government, which sought to take over more and more land.

And while most of the world experienced serious financial problems during the Great Depression, Japan was one of a few countries that actually prospered. The country was exporting many items to other countries.

Its military was growing and becoming more powerful and Japanese influence over Asia began to grow.

Bushido

These factors led to a growing sense of nationalism, or pride, in the country. The nation adopted a code known as *Bushido,* or the "Way of the Warrior." Many people started to believe that it was Japan's destiny to become the most powerful nation—and military—in the world.

Determined to be on the same level with other powerful military nations, the country was unafraid to use its military might, especially against weaker opponents like China.

These feelings of pride and nationalism eventually gave way to another philosophy, one that would destroy Japan at the end of World War II. The people were encouraged to believe that they were protected by gods.

It did not stop there. Before long the people of Japan began to worship their leader, the emperor, as being the center of all power and even as an immortal god himself. They believed the emperor could do no wrong, make no wrong decision, and that he would never allow the country to lose in battle.

Following a Father's Footsteps

The Japanese people believed they were a people of destiny. It was against that backdrop that Murakami's parents were born.

DESTINY

Emperor Akihito delivers a speech in 2013. In the past, emperors were considered gods by the Japanese people.

The Emperor as a God?

When Emperor Hirohito signed papers saying Japan surrendered to the United States in 1945, part of the agreement included him making a public confession to the Japanese people. It was a shocking declaration that he would make on January 1, 1946 over the radio for all to hear.

He was not a god.

Hirohito asked the citizens of Japan to reject the "false conception that the Emperor is divine and that the Japanese people are superior to other races." The Japanese people cried, not wanting to believe his words. He then said to his wife: "Do you see any difference? Do I look more human to you now?"[1]

For centuries, the Japanese people had come to believe that the leader who sat in the emperor's chair was a descendant of the sun goddess Amaterasu. Hirohito, who was the 124th emperor in Japan's history, kept his title until his death in 1989.

When Hirohito surrendered and admitted that he was only a man, it was the first time his voice had been broadcast over the radio in Japan. There were some who were so upset by his surrender that they attacked his palace, but they were quickly defeated. Upon his death, Hirohito's son then became emperor. Not a god, just an emperor.

DESTINY

His father, Chiaki, the son of a Buddhist priest, grew up in a thoughtful and spiritual environment. Their home had its own ornate temple where the family would honor its ancestors, those who came before. It was a very old and revered structure. Honoring the past and showing respect to those who came before you was a very important function of everyday Japanese life.

In Japanese culture, Buddhist priests and family temples hold very important positions in everyday life. Becoming a priest is one of the most respected career paths someone can follow in Japan.

That is probably one of the reasons why, for a while, Chiaki considered following his father's footsteps to become a priest himself. He studied for the priesthood and actually practiced as a Kyoto Buddhist priest for a few years before deciding to follow his one true love: Japanese literature. So, Murakami's father eventually left the priesthood for another noble profession—teacher.

His mother's journey to teaching Japanese literature took a different course. Born the daughter of a merchant in Osaka, Miyuki was raised amidst the hustle and bustle of Japan's third largest city.

Osaka is a large port city on the Japanese island of Honshu where the merchant class is the overwhelming majority. There are numerous historical sites in Osaka including shogun castles and relics of Japan's glory days. The city was established in 1889 and today boasts some of Japan's most modern buildings and architecture.

Murakami's parents' lives would be shaped—as most Japanese citizens were—by the unthinkable: Japan was defeated in World War II. Not only was the Japanese army defeated, but now it was clear that the emperor was not a god, and he had made a terrible mistake by leading the country into a disastrous war.

Living With Bad Memories

The defeat after the United States dropped two atom bombs, not only crushed a nation's spirit but made people question just about everything they had held sacred. Maybe the emperor was not a god after all. Maybe it was not Japan's destiny to rule the world and expand its empire. Maybe the future was not so bright.

Murakami's father was very intelligent. He attended the finest schools, and while he was enrolled in graduate school at Kyoto University, Japan invaded China and he was drafted into the military.

He rarely spoke of his experiences fighting in China, but Murakami would later say that it must have had a terrible impact on his father, who seemed burdened by the memories.

Every morning, Chiaki would kneel at the small Buddhist altar inside their home in the kitchen and offer long, emotional prayers. He told Haruki once that he was praying for those who died during the battles he participated in. He explained that it wasn't enough to pray for the Japanese soldiers who died but also for the Chinese soldiers who lost their lives.

DESTINY

The city of Nagasaki was devastated after the United States dropped an atomic bomb on it to end World War II.

Those words would have a lasting impact on his son. "Staring at his back as he knelt at the altar, I seemed to feel the shadow of death hovering around him,"[2] Murakami would say years later.

Murakami's parents married while American forces occupied Japan and assisting in rebuilding efforts. It was a confusing time. The young couple was living in Kyoto, which had served as the imperial capital of the Japanese empire. This had a profound effect on the mentality of the nation, and it could be one of the reasons why Murakami's parents immersed themselves in the world of Japanese literature. They studied and taught Japanese literature at the high school level, savoring the country's past through eighth-century poetry or tales of medieval battles and bravery. It was a way of holding on to how things used to be before World War II.

Many of the stories dealt with themes like bravery and redemption and held strongly to the notion that warriors were meant to be idolized. One of the most well-known pieces of literature from this time is called *The Tale of the Heike.*

The epic story was originally told by monks traveling from place to place until it was eventually written down. The tale weaves together epic samurai battles and warriors along with a love story. It, along with many other Japanese classics, has been translated into English.

The Rebuilding of a Nation

After the Japanese surrendered to the allied forces in World War II, there was a ton of work to be done. The firebombing of Tokyo plus the atomic bombs dropped on Hiroshima and Nagasaki left much of the country's infrastructure in rubble.

Allied forces, comprised mainly of American military personnel, occupied Japan from 1945 through 1952. They were led by decorated American general Douglas A. MacArthur. Great Britain, China, and Russia also participated in the rebuilding of Japan.

There were basically three phases of Japan's occupation. The first phase dealt with punishing Japanese war criminals and reforming the country's way of thinking. The second phase involved reviving the Japanese economy. The third phase was to make Japan an ally of the United States. This was the first time in Japan's history that foreign troops were on their soil.

In addition to actually rebuilding homes, roads, hospitals, and schools, the most pressing problem was the lack of food. Crops had gone bad and there was a real shortage of food. That's why the first thing MacArthur did was establish an emergency food network. Even with millions of dollars worth of food being shipped in from the allied nations, people in Japan were on the brink of starvation for years.

The ultimate goal was to transform Japan from a militaristic nation to a democracy where the citizens elect their leaders. But food was the initial priority. After all, it is difficult to teach democracy to starving people.

Haruki Murakami: Best-Selling Author

Japanese literature was dominated by epic tales of bravery, battles, and romance, as depicted on this screen.

Starting a Family

The young married couple would spend many nights discussing their favorite works or themes in literature when Miyuki became pregnant with her only son. This would mean the end of her teaching career. In Japanese culture in the 1940s—as it was in the United States—women often stopped working in order to raise children and take care of the house. But Murakami's mother would always relish in her love of literature and the power of words.

US troops stationed in Japan after World War II brought western culture to the country. Haruki Murakami was fascinated and strongly influenced by American music and literature.

The male-dominated society, in which men basically made the rules, was something that Murakami would come to hate. It was also something that he vowed to change in his own personal life. "My father had dominated our family," Murakami said during a 1992 interview. "Japan is a country ruled by men. I hate the situation."[3]

When Haruki was born, on January 12, 1949, the Japan of his parents and his ancestors no longer existed. The world had changed almost overnight and many men like his father, had to deal with the terrible things they had seen during the war.

Haruki would have a totally different life experience. He grew up watching American soldiers and was exposed to people from all over the world, who brought with them a Western culture that included everything from pop music to pulp fiction novels.

And much to the dismay of his parents, the young boy couldn't get enough.

Chapter 3

REBELLING

The theme of water seems to come up over and over again in Murakami's books. The symbolism sometimes means rebirth or cleansing. But more often than not, the theme of water symbolizes a feeling of being trapped for the famous Japanese author. He often uses the imagery of being trapped in water at the bottom of a well. It's no surprise that the author clings to the oldest memory he has.

Murakami's Earliest Memory

At the age of three, Murakami somehow unlocked and opened the front door to his family's home and wandered outside. Unseen by anyone, the little boy waddled across the street, drawn by the sound of water. There in front of him was a running creek. He wanted to get closer and reached down to touch the water, but he lost his balance and fell in.

The fast-moving water carried him downstream. He bobbed under the water a few times and was headed for a long, dark, and scary tunnel. Suddenly, as if out of nowhere, a hand reached down and plucked the little boy from the icy water and possible death.

It was his mother. She clutched him tightly, dried him off, and brought him back inside the house. "I remember it very clearly," he said. "The coldness of the water and the darkness of the tunnel—the shape of that darkness. It's scary. I think that's why I'm attracted to darkness."[1]

The terrible memory would later belong to a character in Murakami's book *The Wind-Up Bird Chronicle*. Looking back now, what seemed like a rushing, dangerous creek and a dark, terrifying tunnel was really no more than water in a gully that was headed for a culvert. Still, to a child, the traumatic experience made a lifelong lasting impression.

Aside from the near-drowning episode, which continues to haunt Murakami to this day, he had a loving and tender childhood by all accounts.

Childhood

Murakami was born in Kyoto but shortly afterward, his family moved to Nishinomiya and then to the outskirts of Kobe, a big city. The home was close to the ocean and had a gorgeous view of the mountains. It was actually quite picturesque and would serve as the backdrop for many of his future stories. His father would one day

Rebelling

Murakami was raised in Kobe, Japan's sixth-largest city. Kobe enjoyed a long tradition of exposure to Western culture.

tell a newspaper reporter that he tried to give his son everything he ever wanted.

And, laughing, he thinks he only failed once. Like many young children, Murakami continuously asked to have a pony when he was a young child. But the family could not afford one, nor did they have a place to keep the animal.

Kobe, Japan's sixth largest city, had always been known as a port city where trade with Western nations took place. But while Murakami was growing up, the city transformed into a cosmopolitan metropolis where the young boy was exposed to Western culture on an everyday basis.

Summer Memories

Murakami described it as a comfy place to experience his childhood. And the theme of a hometown and the nostalgic ties to it is also something that appears often in Murakami's writings.

When he turned five, Murakami started attending Kōroen Elementary School, where he was an average student. And despite the terrible memory of falling into the creek, the little boy became a very good swimmer and spent most of his afternoons swimming at the beach. Some of his fondest memories were spent at the shore, cooling off in the salty water.

During the summer he would run barefoot from his home to the shore. He also loved to go "shrimping" and to explore the vast wooded areas between his home and

Kobe

The large port city of Kobe sits on Osaka Bay in central Japan. The long, narrow city sits between the water and picturesque mountains. Its proximity to the water and shipping lanes helped make Kobe a top port city, meaning they can accommodate many ships from other areas of Japan as well as other countries. It is the fourth busiest port in all of Japan. This made Kobe important in regard to commerce and trade for many years. It also means that Kobe, unlike many other Japanese cities, has a steady stream of foreigners coming in and out of the city.

Today the city is the home of such well-known companies as ASICS and Kawasaki. But it is a cut of expensive steak, Kobe beef, that the city is best-known for. The beef comes from a special type of cattle known as Tajima from Wagyu breed. The meat is known for its tenderness and full flavor.

The funny thing is that when cattle were first introduced to Japan they were used only to pull plows to help with growing rice. These cattle were eventually bred with European cattle and the results are the prized and much sought-after Wagyu cattle that provides the Kobe beef.

The city was one of the allied targets during World War II and was subject to being fire-bombed near the end of the war. The bombing raids destroyed more than twenty percent of the city and killed thousands of its residents.

the beach. It was when he really first let his imagination run wild.

He also enjoyed going to a Shinto shrine every day and paying respect to the ancestors and praying.

Before he was finished with elementary school, Murakami took an entrance exam to the very prestigious Kōyō Gakuin junior high school that his parents wanted him to attend, but he failed. There are two stories surrounding the failed test and only Murakami himself knows which one is true. And he is not likely to spill the beans.

Shinto shrines are often located near peaceful nature sites. As a boy, Murakami visited a Shinto shrine every day to remember those who had come before.

Shinto

Shinto is the main religion for the majority of people in Japan. The word actually means the "way of gods." The religion is based on numerous public shrines that are dedicated to honoring any of the numerous Shinto gods. Unlike many of the world's formal religions, there are no set rituals or services that the people practice. The gods themselves are more like spirits that are everywhere.

For example, the Japanese find great comfort in natural things of beauty like mountains, waterfalls, the ocean, and beautiful trees to name a few. It is believed that the spirits of the gods are contained in those peaceful objects. That is why it is common to see Japanese Shinto shrines near beautiful and peaceful sites.

In keeping with the theme of peace and nature, the religion is based on the natural way of living. They believe honesty and purity—like nature—are the way people should live. They also believe that doing bad things can make a person impure or the very opposite of what a person should strive to be.

Two of the Shinto gods, the male Izanagi and the female Izanami are credited with creating the island nation of Japan. The story goes that the duo was stirring the water with spears when the water that dripped from the end of the spears became land. They lived on this land and built a tremendous palace in the center. Their eight children became the main eight islands of Japan and a nation was born.

One story is that he failed the test miserably even though his teachers—who knew his parents—inflated his score. Another story is that Murakami did not want to go to that school so he erased all of his answers after taking the test and purposely filled in the wrong responses.

The teacher who proctored the exam lived on the same street as Murakami's family and tried to avoid his father for as long as he could. He did not want to deliver the bad news.

Eventually he did break the bad news to Murakami's parents and the youngster then had to attend Seido Municipal Junior High School. From all accounts it was a miserable time in the young boy's life. He would write essays later in life that the teachers in the school followed the old ways. What he meant is that they still taught in the military style before as they did before Japan's defeat in the war. The school, in his eyes, was a dictatorship ruled by cruel people.

Unhappy Student

Murakami did not respond to their strict, regimented style of teaching. He began to rebel in the only way he really knew how: He stopped caring about school. He wrote that the teachers were malicious and would often hit him if he had not studied. The idea of a teacher striking a student seems very strange to us today but this was sometimes the case in most countries, including the United States.

Rebelling

This made Murakami very rebellious and he would often not study on purpose. The beatings at school continued. "My life was forced to bring a substantial change due to the beating from teachers," Murakami said, "It never happened at the elementary school or high school."[2]

During this time period, Murakami became quiet and kept to himself, a theme that would time and time again pop up in his novels. He became an introvert, keeping his thoughts and feelings to himself. Many of his main characters would be described as loners and have to deal with isolation. Like many great writers, Murakami would draw upon his painful childhood experiences to create great characters and scenes for his books.

The family lived a comfortable but modest lifestyle, going out once a week for steak dinners and regularly going to the movie theater. They were not rich, but they were certainly better off than many who were still struggling to cope with life in postwar Japan.

A Disdain for Japanese Literature

His parents would spend their evenings discussing famous Japanese books and their favorite classics at the dinner table. And while their love of reading would eventually rub off on their young son, their love of Japanese history and literature did not. In fact, it had the opposite desired effect: Murakami began to hate it.

Maybe it was just too much. After all, his father would give his son private lessons on Japanese literature every Sunday afternoon. It became stifling. "Throughout my

Haruki Murakami: Best-Selling Author

Murakami did not thrive under the traditional Japanese methods of instruction. He also disliked traditional Japanese literature.

teens I began to hate Japanese literature and teachers," he would later say.[3]

But there would be a place where he could escape his problems and the pressure from his parents. It was a world they would not understand but one that would someday yield one of Japan's greatest writers. He would discover that place, along with other magical escapes, during his high school years.

Chapter 4

WESTERN INFLUENCE

Even before his high school years, Haruki Murakami discovered a place where he could escape the cruelty of his teachers, the pressure of his parents to follow in their footsteps, and even the pressure every middle school student faces in trying to fit in and become popular.

That place was in the pages of some of the world's best-known and most beloved novels and short stories. When he was only twelve years old, Murakami went to the local bookstore and ordered two entire libraries or collections of world literature classics.

Reading the Classics

Every month a different book would arrive at the store and Murakami would run there after school to pick it up and devour the words on the pages. While his parents would rather he had immersed himself in Japanese

Western Influence

literature instead of the Russian, Greek, American, and English greats, they were happy that he spent so much time reading. In truth he simply loved to read, letting his imagination join the characters in some of the greatest stories ever told on their adventures.

In between reading these classic books, Murakami became friends with the owner of the bookstore. The owner would eventually allow Murakami to buy books on credit—meaning he could pay for them later—as long as they were not comic books or weekly magazines about Japanese celebrities. The American and English books were more expensive because they had been translated into Japanese.

The no-comic book rule was just fine with Murakami. Some of his favorite books and authors, the ones that would influence him later in life, included the following: *The Castle*, by Franz Kafka, *The Catcher in the Rye*, by J. D. Salinger, *The Brothers Karamazov*, by Fyodor Dostoyevsky, *The Great Gatsby*, by F. Scott Fitzgerald, and all of the "Philip Marlowe," novels by suspense writer Raymond Chandler.

Marlowe was a tough private eye, a character who really appealed to Murakami. "Philip Marlowe is Chandler's fantasy, but he's real to me. Partly, he made me," Murakami said during an interview with a British newspaper, explaining how Chandler allowed him to get through tough times in school. "I just wanted to live like Marlowe."[1]

Haruki Murakami: Best-Selling Author

Raymond Chandler's detective novels were among Murakami's favorites. Murakami favored British and American literature.

Western Influence

Phillip Marlowe

The tough-as-nails, wisecracking private detective Philip Marlowe, created by American novelist Raymond Chandler, was a fun but complicated character who would inspire Murakami for years.

Even though Chandler portrayed Marlowe as a rough character, he also had a very soft side. He would play chess and recite poetry on occasion. The stories always seemed to center around some betrayal and there was always a femme fatale—a beautiful, yet dangerous woman who tried to steer Marlowe away from the truth and solving the case.

The private detective was first introduced to the world in 1939 in the now classic Raymond Chandler novel, *The Big Sleep*.

Chandler started writing crime stories for *Black Mask* magazine using several different tough-guy characters. Eventually he decided to combine these characters and create Marlowe. He became the star character is such great books as *Farewell, My Lovely* and *The Long Goodbye*

Chandler would say that the writings of Dashiell Hammett, who created the memorable character Sam Spade, served as his inspiration. Marlowe was always quick with his wit and ready with a memorable line. Chandler's use of snappy dialogue and quick conversations set the pace for the books and made them quick reads.

There were several movies made that featured the hard-boiled detective. He was probably best portrayed by terrific American actors Humphrey Bogart and Robert Mitchum. The popular 1970s American television show, *The Rockford Files*, featuring private detective Jim Rockford, is believed to be a modern-day version of Marlowe.

To Murakami, the action, fantasy stories were such a stark contrast to the Japanese literature his father wanted him to read. He didn't care for the Japanese authors, like Yasunari Kawabata—who once won the Nobel Prize for Literature. He felt that Japanese authors cared more about the rhythm or lyrical nature of their stories than the fantasies or adventures that interested him. Murakami was always more interested in the story.

When he wasn't immersed in one of Kafka's impossible situations or trying to figure out who the killer was in the latest Raymond Chandler novel, Murakami fell in love with another Western cultural phenomenon. And once again his parents were not pleased.

A New Sound Called Rock and Roll

Murakami discovered and could not get enough of American music. When he was in middle school it was the new craze called rock-and-roll music. It drove his parents batty.

In a way, Murakami's love of Western culture, literature, and music was not so much a rejection of their Japanese equivalents but maybe just a rejection of Japanese culture before the devastation of World War II. He never wanted to look back at how things were before the war. He was only interested in how things were after the country was rebuilt.

He listened to American music on his radio from the minute he got home from school to the minute he went to bed. He loved the new and very different sounds from recording artists like Elvis Presley and the Beach Boys.

Western Influence

He would spend his allowance—however much was left after buying his precious books—to buy the latest rock-and-roll records from America.

A character in one of his books calls rock-and-roll the greatest thing ever invented. And Murakami has called music an "indispensable" part of his life. Even today, Murakami says he likes to listen to the American rock band Creedence Clearwater Revival as he goes running, when he's not listening to the latest jazz recording.

A New Style

His exposure to Western culture through books and music inspired a big change in Murakami's appearance during high school. He started dressing differently, wearing fancy button-down shirts and polished black shoes. He also grew his hair long, which was very uncommon for Japanese men at the time. His parents tolerated his new style.

Murakami attended one of the best high schools in the area, Kobe High School, but never really applied himself. When he attended classes, he usually spent the time reading a new novel he had just purchased instead of listening to his professor.

By this time, the city of Kobe had a number of secondhand bookstores, and many of them contained English language novels that had been left behind by foreign visitors to the city. They cost less than half the price of the Japanese translations. He started reading books in English, and his command of the language

Haruki Murakami: Best-Selling Author

Teenaged Murakami loved the American sound. He couldn't resist the swagger of Elvis Presley.

grew and grew. This would come in handy years later when Murakami sat down to write his first book.

A New Discovery

Instead of school, Murakami preferred to spend his time playing a popular Asian game called mahjong, which is similar to dominoes. He also started skipping classes to spend time with girls he liked, going to see Western films at the movie theater, smoking cigarettes, and going to jazz clubs to listen to his favorite artists.

The same year that he entered high school was the year Murakami discovered jazz. He was only fifteen when he attended his first jazz concert. His parents bought him a ticket to the concert for his birthday. He went to see Art Blakely and the Jazz Messengers at a live show in 1964 and he was instantly hooked. "This was the first time I really listened to jazz, and it bowled me over. I was thunderstruck," he said, adding that it may have helped inspire him to write years later. "I wondered if it might be possible for me to transfer that music into writing. That was how my style got started."[2]

Murakami would later say that writing and music both need a rhythm and a strong melody. Some of his favorite artists included such jazz greats as Chet Baker, Stan Getz, Charlie "Bird" Parker, and Miles Davis. He loved how at times the music seemed chaotic, out of control, and free, and then just as quickly it would return to some sort of form. Murakami equated it with freedom.

Jazz

Jazz is a style of music that was invented or originated in the United States. It started mainly in African-American communities and is a blending of several different types of music.

Musical experts say jazz began as a combination of European music featuring complicated harmonies, American pop music, brass band music, and the African-American ragtime music.

Jazz is known around the world as one of America's greatest original art forms. The music features syncopated beats, improvisation, and the use of notes not typical in certain keys, known as dissonant sounds.

Over the course of time, different areas of the country and different time periods adopted and put their stamp on jazz, giving it many different styles. For example, there is New Orleans jazz, which features a lot of brass—trumpets, trombones, and tubas among other instruments—blues, and improvisation.

There is also the more structured big-band jazz that became popular in 1930s dance halls and parties. There was also Kansas City jazz, a combination of swing and blues music. Dixieland jazz and swing were also different types of jazz.

Years later even more musical genres would combine, such as gospel music and jazz as well as rock music and jazz, which many refer to as fusion. Today there are numerous forms including Latin jazz, free-form jazz, modal jazz, Afro-Cuban jazz, and even smooth jazz, which is played on easy listening radio stations.

Western Influence

He started skipping lunch at school and using that money to buy the latest jazz records, going hungry in order to listen to the music he loved.

Even though he wasn't a great student, Murakami was still intelligent enough to pass all of his classes and even get average grades. Of course this irritated his parents who knew that he could have been at the top of his class if he paid attention in school and spent any time at all studying.

When his high school graduation arrived, Murakami's grades were not good enough to get him into any of the

The wholly original sounds of jazz musicians like Miles Davis inspired Murakami's career path in unexpected ways. He has said he writes in a jazz style.

country's top colleges. He was good at English, from all of his reading, as well as social studies and history. But his downfall was science, a subject that was a real struggle for him. Still, Murakami decided that he would try to attend law school and become a lawyer, which made his parents happy. But that happiness would not last for long.

Chapter 5

FINDING HIS WAY

Haruki Murakami might have been just trying to make his family happy when he announced that he wanted to go to law school. Without much preparation, he failed the law school entrance exam after graduating high school.

But, in his defense, the exam is especially difficult, and most high school graduates fail it on their first attempt. So, he announced he would take the exam again the following year.

This time he studied. He spent the majority of 1967 at the Ashiya Library with his head buried in law books and examination preparation books. But, unfortunately the result was no different the second time around. He failed again and his parents, especially his father, were very disappointed.

Haruki Murakami: Best-Selling Author

For a time, it seemed as if Murakami was headed for failure. His parents didn't understand his interests or lifestyle.

Rising From Failure

Of course, these failures would one day open the door for Murakami to become one of the most-beloved authors in the world. This was a tough time in the Murakami household. Father and son were often butting heads about just about everything. They argued about Murakami's long hair, his late nights hanging out at jazz clubs, his obsession with American music, and literature from the Western world. But most of all, they argued about the young man's future.

What was he going to do with his life? Murakami would later say that he hated disappointing his father and that it affected him greatly as a boy and young man. He wanted to be the person his father wanted him to be but was unable to accomplish that.

Murakami eventually decided to go with his passion, which must have pleased his parents somewhat. He took and passed the exam to get into the prestigious Department of Literature program at Waseda University in Tokyo. This institution of higher learning is regarded as one of the best private universities in all of Japan and has produced many of the country's best writers and journalists.

His father held out hope that Murakami would finally embrace Japanese literature. Maybe he would become a writer, editor, or even follow in his father's footsteps and teach literature, an honorable profession.

Writing Careers

Murakami's father was happy when his son finally settled on a college that specialized in a literature and writing program. He thought it would finally offer his son a chance to choose a career and settle down.

There are many careers available to people who studied there. One of them is journalism. Journalism careers include reporters, editors, copy editors, and designers. Reporters are the men and women who go out to seek and report about the news. This can be print, like in a newspaper or website, or broadcast journalism, which includes television, radio, and podcasts.

The people who verify some of the factual information and make sure the words written or spoken are impactful as well as grammatically correct are the editors. There are also assignment editors, who direct the reporters and tell them what stories to cover.

Copy editors offer another layer of editing, reading stories, verifying facts, and correcting mistakes before the story goes to the page designer. These are the people who organize the pages of a newspaper or a website to make sure they look good and are easily accessible to someone who wants the news.

In today's world, journalism has evolved to include blogs, cell-phone videos and even citizen journalism and social media sites like Twitter.

Of course, other careers include teaching and creative writing, the path that Murakami would eventually take to the delight of many around the world.

An Unsure Future

But that was not meant to be either. Murakami gravitated more toward drama, which he studied at school while working at his first job—a record store. Sometimes this did not work out well as he would spend most of his paycheck buying the latest jazz recordings. He became more and more interested in music. During this period he grew his hair even longer and he even grew out a beard.

If his future seemed uncertain or cloudy it is only because Murakami spent time trying to please his father. But eventually he had the self-confidence to do the things he wanted and pursue his own dreams. He would later say that it was only because he was certain of the things that made him happy. "Confidence; as a teenager? Because I knew what I loved. I loved to read; I loved to listen to music; and I love cats," he said. "Those three things. So, even though I was an only kid, I could be happy because I knew what I loved. Those three things haven't changed from my childhood. I know what I love, still, now. That's a confidence. If you don't know what you love, you are lost."[1]

It was also during his time at college that he met a young woman named Yoko. The couple fell in love and despite a lot of uncertainty about their future, they were sure of one thing: They wanted to be together. She loved that he treated her as his equal, something that had not always been the case in Japanese relationships.

Haruki Murakami: Best-Selling Author

Even though he had not yet completed his studies at the university, the young rebellious man once again disappointed his father by not working in his field of study. In fact, he never even tried to find a job. Instead, against his parents' wishes, the young couple got married and borrowed a lot of money from the bank in order to open up their very own jazz club in Tokyo!

Murakami met his wife, Yoko, while the two were attending college. Further confounding his traditional parents, Haruki and Yoko opened a jazz club in Tokyo.

Tokyo

The bustling city marked by neon lights and ultramodern architecture featuring breathtaking skyscrapers known as Tokyo is the capital of Japan. It not only is the largest city in all of Japan, but is the most populous city in the world. That means more people live in it than any other city, with more than thirteen million people calling Tokyo home. It is also the most expensive place to live in the world.

The city has come a long way from the tiny fishing village it once was that known as Edo.

Tokyo is situated on the southeastern side of the main island of Japan and the word Tokyo actually means "to east." It may not have been officially the capital, but the city has been home to the government since the early 1600s. It became the official capital of Japan in 1868.

The city suffered widespread destruction during World War II when the allies dropped firebombs on the city and destroyed nearly 300,000 structures. But the entire city was rebuilt and made better than ever.

Tokyo contains numerous small cities as well as small islands just off the coast. The climate of Tokyo is similar to that of Florida in the United States. It is hot and humid throughout the year with temperatures that exceed 100 degrees Fahrenheit during the summer months.

The city is known as a center of business with many big companies boasting offices and headquarters there. But it is also a major tourist destination. Visitors come to Tokyo to enjoy the culture as well as numerous museums, theaters, festivals, and some of the best cooking in the world.

Making Himself Happy

His parents protested both the young marriage and going into debt to buy a jazz club. Murakami had long ago fallen in love with jazz music and even considered learning to play a musical instrument and becoming a jazz musician himself. But after realizing that he would never be able to master an instrument, he decided the next best thing would be to live his life surrounded by the music he loved.

He wanted to make himself happy and music certainly did. Looking back now, Murakami realizes that he took many chances with his future as a young man. He knows things could have ended badly if his gambles had not paid off. "It was so exciting, but at the same time, it was risky. The bets were so big. If you can win, you could get big bets, but if you lose, you are lost," he said, explaining that he took chances by opening the bar and marrying at such a young age. "Marriage is where I took that gamble! I was 20 or 21. I didn't know anything of the world. I was stupid. Innocent. It's a kind of a gamble. With my life. But I survived. Anyway."[2]

He has done more than survive. The couple is still married and his wife, Yoko, is the first person who reads and critiques whatever he writes. Their relationship is a clear break from the traditional Japanese male-dominated household that he grew up in. "We've been married for 40 years or something. She's still my friend," he told a reporter from *The Guardian*. "We have a conversation, always a conversation. She helps me a lot. She gives me advice regarding my books. I respect her opinion. Sometimes we quarrel. Her opinion is so harsh sometimes. It can be."[3] He joked that he can fire an editor if he is unhappy with the comments, but he can't fire his wife.

He used his love of music and his love of cats as inspiration for the name for his club. He named the jazz club "The Peter Cat," and ran it with his wife. He once owned a cat named Peter and today even says that whenever he sees a cat it makes him happy.

It was very difficult to run a bar and book music. They worked many hours a day and very late into the night. He would do it all—from sweeping the floors, to mixing drinks, to making sandwiches and handling the money and finances. But running the club was something the young couple loved to do, and eventually Murakami's parents accepted what their son had chosen to do with his life.

Plus, despite the long hours and hard work, eventually the club started making some money. It seemed as if he was set in his career at last: jazz club owner. And in a way, he used the club to isolate himself from the outside world and the pressures of having to find a traditional job and live the life that was expected of him. The music, the club, the atmosphere became his escape. "I was a hermit in a wonderland of jazz," he said.[4] That wonderland would last for about a decade into the 1970s.

Murakami often dreamt of being a great musician because of his love of music, but he never dared to dream of being a writer, despite his love of books, until he decided to spend a spring evening watching a local baseball game. Because, like many of his books, the unexpected can border on being absurd.

Chapter 6

BASEBALL

Anyone who loves baseball will tell you there is magic in the game. There is something about the distance between bases, between the pitcher and batter, that seems symmetrically perfect. There is a sweetness watching parents and their children at the ballpark. There is an enviable camaraderie between the men on the field and in the dugout pulling for each other. The grass never seems greener, the clay never seems redder, and the air never seems as fresh as when you are at a baseball game. It is a place of magic.

But for Haruki Murakami, the magic became so real it would absolutely change his life forever. Those who believe in the wonder and magic of baseball would not think it was coincidental that the first Japanese player to participate in a Major League Baseball game in the United States was named Mansori Murakami in 1964!

Japanese Baseball

While there were already games that involved a bat and ball in France and in Great Britain, the game of baseball—as we know it today—was invented in the United States.

The earliest reports of the game being played in the United States are from the late 1700s, shortly after the country won its independence from Britain. For many years the game was thought to be invented by Abner Doubleday in 1839, but that has been proven false in recent years.

American soldiers brought the sport of baseball anywhere they were stationed. But even though many Americans stayed on to restore the country and help the people rebuild after the war, the Japanese were already playing the game. It was introduced by American teacher Horace Wilson in 1872.

Six years later there was already an established team and the love affair between the Japanese and baseball was on. It became wildly popular in the 1920s and 1930s when professional leagues brought the sport to the country's major cities.

Baseball is so popular and has been played for so long in Japan that fans are sometimes surprised to hear that it is America's national sport.

Over the years many of Japan's top stars have made the jump to play in the US. Japanese teams only allow four foreign players—mainly Americans—on their rosters. Usually the Americans that wind up playing in Japan are at the tailend of their playing careers.

Japan has won the World Baseball Classic—a tournament held every four years among the countries of the world—twice since its inception in 2006.

BASEBALL

The man known as the "Japanese Jackie Robinson" is not related to Haruki Murakami.

Destiny

It was opening day in April 1978 when twenty-nine-year-old Haruki Murakami sat in the stands on a humid night to watch Tokyo's baseball team, the Yakult Swallows, take on the visiting Hiroshima Toyo Carp. He sometimes went for long walks, and sometimes those long walks took him past the baseball stadium.

The Swallows had not been very good for several years, and there were not many fans in attendance. Murakami sat with no one around him in the outfield grandstands. He bought a beer and stretched his legs out to enjoy the game.

The game took on a little bit of added interest because the Swallows had signed an American baseball player, Dave Hilton, to a contract. This was before the widespread crossover you see now with Japanese players in the United States and American players on Japanese teams.

But Hilton, who had played a few unspectacular seasons with the San Diego Padres, decided he needed a change. He wrote letters to every Japanese team asking for a tryout. A scout with the Swallows met him in Arizona and liked what he saw. The team signed him to a contract.

It was during the bottom of the first inning that Hilton came to bat against Hiroshima's starting pitcher Yoshiro Sotokoba. Hilton swung at the very first pitch

Haruki Murakami: Best-Selling Author

The crack of a baseball bat at a Yakult Swallows game was like a lightbulb going off in Murakami's head.

and with the crack of the bat he lined a double into the left field corner.

That was the moment everything changed for a twenty-nine-year-old jazz club owner who happened to be sitting in the stands. Murakami would describe the moment in the introduction to his novel *Hear the Wind Sing*.

> The satisfying crack when the bat met the ball resounded throughout Jingu Stadium. Scattered applause rose around me. In that instant, for no reason and on no grounds whatsoever, the thought suddenly struck me: I think I can write a novel.
>
> I can still recall the exact sensation. It felt as if something had come fluttering down from the sky, and I had caught it cleanly in my hands. I had no idea why it had chanced to fall into my grasp. I didn't know then, and I don't know now. Whatever the reason, it had taken place. It was like a revelation. Or maybe epiphany is the closest word. All I can say is that my life was drastically and permanently altered in that instant—when Dave Hilton belted that beautiful, ringing double at Jingu Stadium.[1]

A Crystallizing Moment

Murakami has told the story numerous times. Out of the blue, once Hilton hit that ball, Murakami believed he should and would be a writer. Suddenly this voracious reader had a new calling. While the idea of someone deciding to change careers so drastically after an event as simple as a base hit in baseball may seem strange or magical to most of us, it did not surprise a professor with the University of Pennsylvania whose specialty is analyzing the creative mind.

"It's actually called a crystallizing moment," he said during a radio interview. "I think this story is actually kind of a perfect illustration of the situation because it's seemingly such an unrelated event. Yet it's such a common thing when people have the crystallizing experience. It's usually at something where their consciousness has not been actively been trying to figure out what it is they are trying to do."[2]

The Swallows won the baseball game, but Murakami could only think about one thing: trying to write a novel. He took the train after the game to go buy a few packages of paper and a fountain pen. Remember, this was before computers, so everything had to be written by hand.

But Murakami didn't mind. He later explained how excited he was to "put pen to paper." He was still running the jazz club with his wife. But he cleared the kitchen table at their home and that would be his new writing center, whenever he could find the time away from the club. Usually that was late at night or during the early hours of the next day.

Getting Started

Murakami would sit at the table for several hours every night after work. The house was quiet and it even seemed as if the entire city was quiet. He was able to concentrate, but it was not always easy.

For example, his reading list still included American detective novels and Russian epics. He had no idea what

BASEBALL

Having had his crystallizing moment, Murakami set about writing. He sat at his kitchen table nightly to work on his novel.

sorts of books Japanese authors were writing or, more importantly, what the people were reading. He really had no idea how to write a novel, so he was going on sheer guesswork.

He was not impressed, six months later, when he had a short novel called *Hear the Wind Sing*, completed. He thought it was boring. He decided he would take another crack at it, but this time he would write in the style of his own thoughts and words instead of trying to sound more literary or intelligent. He replaced the long, flowery descriptions and sentences with simple, short sentences.

But that would take a drastic step, an experiment really. First, he pulled his old typewriter out of his closet and replaced the sheets and handwritten notes of paper that were on his kitchen table.

Then he thought about how to simplify his words and his sentences. He thought maybe, he could write it in English and then translate it. His thinking was that since his command of the English language was very simple and his English vocabulary was limited that it would force him to keep things simple and get more quickly to the point. Even if the ideas and themes in his head were complex and intricate, the words would be simple. He realized there was no need for difficult words. He came to the conclusion that he would have to write the book for himself instead of trying to impress anyone else.

He describes Japanese language, words, and descriptions as a barn crowded with too many animals.

Baseball

Murakami took a chance and first wrote his novel in English. This allowed him a simpler and more direct style.

Haruki Murakami: Best-Selling Author

Writing in a Different Language

Haruki Murakami's brilliant idea to start out his book in English, which was not his native language, in order to simplify his writing style worked out for him. But he is not the only writer to use this device.

Well-known writer Agota Kristof was born in Hungary but was forced to escape the country's violence and communist rule when she was twenty-one years old. She moved to Switzerland and learned to speak, read, and write French, one of the country's four national languages. Other official languages of Switzerland are German, Italian, and Romansh.

Kristof was working at a job she hated in a factory, but quit after five years and decided to write a novel. Instead of writing in her native Hungarian, she decided to try writing in French.

Her first novel, *The Notebook*, was published in 1986 and is the first part of a popular trilogy. She was recognized with a couple of major writing awards in Europe, and her first book was translated into thirty different languages.

Three of the nine novels she wrote have been translated into English. One of her novels influenced the popular video game "Mother 3." She passed away in 2011 at the age of seventy-five.

He jotted down the opening to his novel in English and then translated it back into his native Japanese. He was stunned to see how much of a difference it had made. The words popped and the writing seemed crisper, more alive. The writing developed a rhythm.

He would later say that writing in a foreign language allowed him to remove the obstacles and limitations that he had placed on his own writing. Once this new "trick" started working, Murakami returned the typewriter to the closet and once again started writing by hand. It just seemed more natural to him.

And just like that, a novelist was born.

Murakami was flattered to be compared to Ernest Hemingway, the great American writer known for his bare style.

Chapter 7

BEST-SELLING AUTHOR

Murakami was pleased with his finished manuscript and sent the only copy he had to *Gunzo*, a Japanese literary magazine that had an annual contest for new writers.

Almost a year passed, and Murakami had forgotten that he had even sent them his book. He had done it, he had written a novel, and now he was back doing what he knew best—operating his jazz club. Writing a book had been exciting, but at the same time it was very draining and so the thirty-year-old Murakami doubted he would ever write another novel.

Then, one lazy Sunday morning when Murakami was trying to catch up on his sleep from working late the night before, he was awakened by the ring of his telephone. It was eleven in the morning, but Murakami was still fast asleep.

By the time he answered the call, he was groggily trying to figure out who was on the other end and what it was all about. Finally, he realized it was the editor from *Gunzo* telling him that *Hear the Wind Sing* was selected as a finalist for their top award.

The book, about people without much direction after their college years, has been compared to the style of great American writer Ernest Hemingway. The action and the characters' feelings are told mainly through dialogue and short, snippy sentences, much like the way Hemingway wrote.

Lost Forever?

Murakami couldn't believe it. He thought no one would ever read the book. Because *Gunzo* only returns winning manuscripts, Murakami thought his book would be lost forever. Now he was one of only five finalists up for the prestigious award.

He was thrilled with the news and remembers going out that morning for a walk with his wife, Yoko.

"If they hadn't selected it, it probably would have vanished forever," he said. "Most likely too, I would have never written another novel. Life is strange."[1]

During the walk with his wife Murakami found an injured carrier pigeon and gently picked it up from the bushes. He cradled the bird to drop it of at the local police station. The warmth of the bird in his hands gave

Best-Selling Author

Ernest Hemingway

Regarded by some as the greatest American writer, "Papa," or Ernest Hemingway, wrote some of the most well-known twentieth-century novels such as *The Sun also Rises*, *A Farewell to Arms*, and *The Old Man and the Sea*.

Born in Illinois in 1899, Hemingway had a thirst for adventure from a very young age. Already an accomplished hunter and fisherman by the time he was a teenager, he volunteered to become an ambulance driver for the Italian army during World War I. The United States had yet to enter the war and he wanted to see what it was like. He suffered an injury, which served as the story line to a *Farewell to Arms*, about a young American ambulance driver who falls in love with a British nurse.

He became a journalist after the war, where he honed his writing skills and learned to write in the short, crisp sentences that Murakami would mirror many years later.

After the war and a short stint back in the United States, Hemingway and his first wife moved to Paris where he became part of what is known as the "Lost Generation," a group of American and British writers and artists living and working together in Paris. That is where he wrote the classic *The Sun Also Rises*.

When he wasn't writing books, Hemingway continued looking for adventure much of his life. He boxed, fished, went big game hunting, reported from wars in numerous places, and went running with the bulls during annual bullfighting festivals in Spain.

Hemingway won the Nobel Peace Prize for Literature for the incredible story *The Old Man and the Sea*.

him a comforting feeling similar to the feeling he had at the baseball game. "I always call up those sensations when I think about what it means to write a novel," he said. "Such tactile memories teach me to believe in that *something* I carry within me, and to dream of the possibilities it offers."[2]

He had a feeling that he would definitely win the award. And he was right! *Gunzo* awarded him their top prize and published his book. Murakami was now a published author.

Critics didn't know what to make of this new novel, *Hear the Wind Sing*, or this new author—Haruki Murakami—who had turned out something very different from what they were used to reading.

Some critics did not like the writing and others called the style an insult to Japanese writing and language. Their observations did not bother him, and Murakami continued to run the Peter Cat Jazz Bar. But now something had changed. Armed with the newfound confidence that his story won a major award, Murakami took the sheaths of paper from his closet and placed them back on the kitchen table.

Back to Work

It was time to get back to work. He tried to dedicate at least one hour every night after working at the club to writing his next novel, *Pinball*, a sort of sequel to his first book and his first attempt at what would be his specialty, the world of magical realism. The book features a weird

Best-Selling Author

Not content to rest on the publication of his first novel, Murakami got right back to work on a second.

set of twins inside a gigantic warehouse filled with noisy pinball machines.

He would in later years refer to these two novels as his "kitchen table fiction." He would also resist having them translated into English because he felt embarrassed about them, though many consider them great pieces of writing. It's just that the books that came later were so much better.

Bye-bye Peter

Once *Pinball* was published and sold many copies, Murakami and his wife had to make a big decision. Would he continue to run a time-consuming jazz bar while also working as a part-time writer, or would he decide to pursue writing on a full-time basis?

The decision was actually an easy one. The couple sold the bar, and Murakami left that life behind to concentrate solely on his writing career. But, he also knew that he would have to live a disciplined life and approach his writing career as if he wanted to be the best writer in the world. That meant centering his entire life around writing.

It has worked out pretty well. For the last thirty years, Murakami has basically followed the same routine. He used to swim long distances every day before becoming a runner. Now he runs several miles a day. He eats healthy food and makes sure he is in bed by 9 P.M.

He wakes up at about 4 A.M., has coffee at his desk, and spends the next six hours writing. He once said during an interview that he sees his desk as a place of

Best-Selling Author

Magical Realism

The theme of magical realism can be found not only in fictional literature, but also in art and movies. The basic idea of magic realism centers on the belief—among the characters in that particular novel or movie—that magic exists in their normal, rational world.

In other words, they are people just like us who may experience a different reality than we normally would. An example of magical realism would be a normal woman who goes to work and raises her children, but maybe has a talking fish. And to her, and those around her, it is completely normal. Normal people are faced with things that most of us would find too strange to believe. It is also sometimes called "fabulism."

Magical realism in literature is thought to have been started by Latin American writers, such as the legendary Gabriel Garcia Marquez, who were inspired by the vast differences in art and culture between their home countries and Europe.

In art, the term was first coined in Germany to refer to a new type of painting that was also called the "new objectivity." In addition to Haruki Murakami, other well-known magical realism authors include Jorge Luis Borges, Anna Castillo, and Salmon Rushdie.

confinement, like a jail, though a happy place at the same time. "Concentration is one of the happiest things in my life," he said. "If you cannot concentrate, you are not so happy. I'm not a fast thinker, but once I am interested in something, I am doing it for many years. I don't get bored. I'm kind of a big kettle. It takes time to get boiled, but then I'm always hot."[3]

Murakami never had children. It wasn't his dedication as a writer that prevented Murakami and his wife from having children and starting a family. It had more to do with the unhappiness he experienced as a child that kept him from ever becoming a father. "(My parents) were just disappointed in me," he said. "It's tough on a kid to have that disappointment. I think they are nice people, but still. I was injured. I remember that feeling, still. I wanted to be a good kid for them, but I couldn't be. Myself, I don't have any kids. Sometimes I wonder what would have happened if I'd had children. I cannot imagine it. I'm not so happy as a kid, and I don't know if I could be happy as a father. I have no idea."[4]

Even after he became a successful and well-respected author, Murakami said his parents doubted the career choice he had made. Those feelings of loneliness and confusion are often themes in his books, including his third book—*A Wild Sheep Chase*—which was the third part of the trilogy of the Rat. The Rat was a character in his first three books. He was a bartender who appears as a supporting character in the three stories.

The switch from jazz club owner to full-time writer paid off. *A Wild Sheep Chase* is considered Murakimi's first great book and many consider it a classic. It was published in 1982, and that same year was awarded the Noma Literary Newcomer's Prize.

Best-Selling Author

Colombian writer Gabriel Garcia Marquez popularized magic realism, a literary style Murakami experimented with in *A Wild Sheep Chase*.

The story combines Murakami's love of American detective novels with magical realism. It revolves around a Japanese detective who begins to look for a certain sheep that has not been seen for many years. There is a woman with magical ears and a man who dresses as a sheep, confusing the investigation.

World Renown

The book became very popular overseas and received great reviews by American critics. Some called it the most important book about postwar Japan ever written even though it is mixes reality and things that cannot be explained—magic.

That, Murakami would later say, was something he came up with while writing. He realized that he could make the characters do anything he wanted. If he wanted a character to suddenly interact with a talking cat or a spirit or have some inexplicable magic powers, he would simply make it happen. His books have included levitating clocks and exploding dogs.

This magical realism would catapult him to the top of the literary world.

Chapter 8

Running to Commercial Success

Haruki Murakami had made it. With every book he wrote the more popular he became. And it really is amazing because, while he always has a general idea of what he wants to write about, Murakami has said that once he begins writing he lets the story take him where it needs to go.

He uses the strategy of asking himself "What If?" For example, the idea for one of his newer books *IQ84* came to him while he was sitting in traffic. He wondered what would happen if he just abandoned his car in the middle of the highway and ran down an exit ramp.

It Just Happens

Of course the story contains elements of magic realism, especially when tiny little people the size of bugs are introduced. Murakami refers to them as "the little people," and says they were not anything he planned. It just sort of happened. "The Little People came suddenly," he said. "I don't know who they are. I don't know what it means. I was a prisoner of the story. I had no choice. They came, and I described it. That is my work."[1] The only time that he did not use that strategy was while writing the modern-day classic *Norwegian Wood*, which is also the title of the famous song by the revolutionary rock band The Beatles, in the 1960s. Murakami was gained the acceptance of critics outside Japan and enjoyed good book sales, but he wanted to write something that could be both popular and a commercial hit. What he wound up with is a fascinating book that many people consider the Japanese version of *The Catcher in the Rye*. It is said that *Norwegian Wood* is a must read for every Japanese teenager.

This is the book that made Murakami very famous in Japan. The book was hailed worldwide. The *New York Times* described it as "masterly," while the *Baltimore Sun* said the book "captured the heartbeat of a generation."

Appealing to Teen Angst

The book is about young people and the constant pressure they are under to fit in and find themselves. Many reviewers and critics said the novel had many autobiographical features, meaning that the main character in the story shares many of the same feelings and experiences as Murakami, especially during his teenage years.

Running to Commercial Success

Murakami's 1987 novel *Norwegian Wood* was adapted into a motion picture in 2010. *Norwegian Wood* was a big hit among Japanese youth, bringing Murakami newfound fame.

Haruki Murakami: Best-Selling Author

The Catcher in the Rye

Haruki Murakami had the pleasure of being hired to translate J. D. Salinger's brooding American novel, *The Catcher in the Rye*, into Japanese. While he has great respect for the work, Murakami felt Salinger could not escape the darkness of his characters, and that is reflected in the book.

Salinger wrote *The Catcher in the Rye*, in 1951, and it is regarded as one of the top American novels of all time. The book deals with teenage angst and belonging, and like Murakami's novels, the main character's story is often said to be closely related to Salinger's own life.

Salinger was ill-prepared for the attention and fame the book would bring him. He shunned the media and his fans and became very reclusive. He lived with his wife and children in a very isolated area in Cornish, New Hampshire and hardly came into contact with others. He even hated talking on the telephone, preferring instead to write letters.

It also affected his writing. He slowed down a bit after the popularity of *The Catcher in the Rye*, and he stopped writing altogether in the mid-1960s. He sued writers and publishers who used his name or tried to write his biography.

Salinger faced a lot of pressure to live up to the success of *The Catcher in the Rye*, and he was never able to achieve that greatness again. He granted no interviews after 1980 and died at the age of ninety-one in 2010. There are rumored to be numerous short stories and other fiction that Salinger wrote that were never published.

There are fewer fantasy elements in the book than many of his other stories, but it still feels very dreamlike and the mood of the writing and the behavior of the characters is sometimes described as otherworldly.

The book sold more than three million copies in Japan when it first came out, and it has been translated into numerous languages and sold all over the world. His popularity around the globe is still something that surprises Murakami to this day as he considers himself just a regular guy who writes. For example, he was stunned when more than 1,000 people attended a book signing for him in Barcelona, Spain. People scrambled to get closer to him, and women even tried to kiss him!

With each passing book, Murakami's popularity around the world grew. So did his life experiences. He lived and wrote in other countries like Italy and the United States, where he was invited to be a visiting professor at prestigious universities.

But above all else, Murakami enjoys his privacy and is never really comfortable speaking in front of large crowds or offering his writing expertise. He remains humble.

But while his world travels, speaking tours, and best-selling books increased his fame and fortune, one thing started to suffer: his health. Murakami thought that smoking cigarettes could help him concentrate better while writing his novels. It got to the point where he was smoking sixty cigarettes a day! Not to mention the cancer and breathing risks involved with smoking so

Haruki Murakami: Best-Selling Author

At the stroke of midnight, excited fans crowded into a Tokyo bookstore to buy the latest Murakami novel.

much, but Murakami's appearance changed as well. His nails and teeth grew yellow from cigarettes. His skin and color were also changed and not in a good way.

Getting Healthy

In 1982 he decided to stop smoking once and for all. While that was a good, healthy step, the result was that he started eating more and became very heavy. "When I decided to stop smoking, at the age of 33, I sprouted rolls of fat on my hips," he said.[2]

He made a decision to get into shape and become more active. But how? There was soccer, tennis, martial arts, and numerous other activities for him to get moving and lose weight. But he did not want to do anything that relied on other people, like a team sport. He wanted to do something that only he had total control of; he only wanted to compete against himself. So he chose running. It did not go very well at first, however. "After 20 minutes I was out of breath, my heart was hammering, my legs were trembling," he said. "At first I was uncomfortable when other people saw me jogging. But I integrated running into my day like brushing my teeth. So I made rapid progress. After just under a year I ran my first, though unofficial, marathon."[3]

A Lonely Life

It is no coincidence that Murakami chose to become a runner. Much like writing, running can be a very lonely endeavor. It takes great willpower to sit in front of a typewriter or computer and force yourself to write every

Completing grueling marathons gives Murakami a sense of satisfaction and accomplishment, much like writing a novel.

single day until the story is complete. The same can be said about running a long distance. The finish line may seem far away, but with every single step it draws that much closer.

He admits to sometimes forcing himself to write every day in order to get into a habit. The same, he said, can be said of running. There are always excuses not to run: too hot, too cold, too cloudy, too rainy. But he always forces himself to do it.

In fact, when he is running, Murakami tries to empty his mind, clearing it of all thoughts so he can simply focus on the next step. Sometimes he speaks to himself in his mind, saying "You can do this. You can do it."

Murakami said while there is great satisfaction in finishing a long race, like a marathon, it does not compare to the feeling he gets when he has written the final word of a novel that he is happy with. "Putting the final full stop at the end of a story is like giving birth to a child, an incomparable moment," he said. A fortunate author can write maybe twelve novels in his lifetime. I don't know how many good books I still have in me; I hope there are another four or five. When I am running I don't feel that kind of limit. I publish a thick novel every four years, but I run a ten-kilometer race, a half-marathon and a marathon every year."[4]

He combined the two passions when he wrote a very powerful and popular memoir called *What I Talk About When I Talk About Running*, in 2007. The book explains his writing and running process. But now the running

Marathons

A marathon is a running race that spans a little bit more than twenty-six miles. While Haruki Murakami tries to run at least one full marathon every year, there is one attempt that he is most proud of.

He flew to Greece in order to run from Athens to Marathon in order to recreate the very first marathon race. Legend has it that a Greek warrior in the town of Marathon fighting against the Persians in 490 BCE was instructed to go to Athens to alert everyone that the Persian army had been defeated.

The messenger supposedly ran all twenty-six miles without stopping even though he had just fought in the battle. He ran into the government chambers and yelled "We have won!" before collapsing and dying right there on the spot.

Whether it is true or not, Murakami decided to try it himself. Through grueling heat he was able to make the run in just under four hours. The sun beat down on him and caused his skin to form small blisters. No one else was making the run, and when he was done, he simply sat down at a gasoline station and had a cold drink. When the owner of the gas station learned what he had done, he presented Murakami with flowers.

Marathons are held all over the world and are also an Olympic sport.

Running to Commercial Success

and the writing go hand in hand and offer more than just physical health benefits. Murakami believes that running has made him a better writer. He explains that sometimes he finds himself in a very dark place in a story that he is writing. He needs to be strong both physically and mentally to be able to deal with it.

He would also have to be strong physically and mentally to deal with a disaster in his native country.

Haruki Murakami: Best-Selling Author

A man stands in front of burnt-out buildings after the devastating earthquake that rocked Murakami's hometown of Kobe in 1995.

Chapter 9

JAPAN'S 9/11

Haruki Murakami already showed his writing depth by moving seamlessly between fiction and nonfiction in his work about the sarin terrorist attack on the Tokyo subway. While he condemned the attackers for what they did, his interviews with them and inclusion of what they had to say in his book *Underground* proved what a complete and thorough writer he is.

Hearing what they had to say had a profound impact on him as well and is reflected in his writing. "It was so sad to listen to the cult people," he said during an interview shortly after the book was published. "There was something missing. They had lost their own reality. They were criticizing the social system of Japan, so they went to the (leader of the attack), who offered a new system. All they did was choose between them; people have got to find their own system. The Japanese system offered a fantasy that the harder you work the richer you get. The (leader of the attack) offered his system, his fantasy and story, so that people could dream. But it was dangerous."[1]

Writing From Real Life

He would later show his skill at fictionalizing a terrible event in Japanese history—the 1995 earthquake in Kobe, Japan. He said he finds disasters, whether they are natural or man-made, to be fascinating topics to write about. In fact, the dark, alternate fantasy life the cult members believed in while planning the gas attack is something that happens often in his dark, dreamlike books.

But there is one major difference. While many of the themes in his books appear hopeless and dark, there is always a lightness or fanciful feel to them. In other words, they are not scary but dark, odd and oftentimes funny. His book, *After the Quake*, is a collection of six short stories that all take place in February of 1995. That was the same month of the earthquake.

All six stories are about fictional events that occurred after the earthquake. Murakami's goal in writing the stories was to show how fragile and how fleeting life can be. A theme in many of his stories is how random and unpredictable life can be. Earthquakes and poison gas attacks fit right into that kind of thinking. But there is also odd humor to be found in the stories and ultimately, even a little bit of hope that life will and does go on.

Japan's 9/11

Japan's 2011 Disaster

The strongest earthquake ever to hit Japan struck on March 11, 2011. It was a magnitude 9.0 earthquake. To put that into context, the earthquake that killed 200,000 in Haiti just a year earlier registered as a 7.0.

The earthquake occurred in the northwest Pacific Ocean and was followed by several strong aftershocks. When there is an earthquake in the ocean, the risk of a tsunami, or giant wave, is increased. Because Japan has very good earthquake warning systems, millions of people were alerted to the quake and many lives were saved.

But many lives were lost as well, especially after the water began to rise. The massive wave struck Japan's coastline within an hour of the earthquake and did not stop there. The water kept coming, carrying houses, trains, and cars along as if they were small toys.

The tsunami was much deadlier than the actual earthquake, and entire towns were wiped off the face of the earth, along with everyone who lived in them. More than 15,000 people were killed.

It got worse. The surging water slammed into a nuclear power plant at Fukushima and caused a meltdown. This happens when radiation escapes. Nearby towns had to be evacuated, and the radiation levels were estimated to be 1,000 times the normal range. It takes years to determine the amount of radioactive damage, but high radiation levels were found in fish and beef years after the meltdown. This is considered one of the worst disasters in Japanese history.

While the writing was genius and helped a nation heal, writing it perhaps prepared Murakami for the tragic and horrendous 2011 earthquake and tsunami that killed so many in his country.

Meltdown

Murakami was living in Hawaii with his wife when the earthquake and tsunami struck. The quake damaged a nuclear power plant and many were exposed to harmful radiation. It became something that was typical of a Murakami novel. But this time it was for real.

Murakami said it changed his country forever. "People lost their confidence," he said during an interview. "We had been working so hard, after the end of the war. For 60 years. The richer we became, the happier we become. But at the end, we didn't get happy, however hard we worked. And the earthquake came, and so many people had to be evacuated, to abandon their houses and homeland. It's a tragedy. And we were proud of our technology, but our nuclear power plant turned out to be a nightmare. So people started to think, we have to change drastically the way of life. I think that is a big turning point in Japan."[2]

He called it Japan's 9/11 event, referring to the September 11, 2001 terrorist attack on the United States by Muslim extremists. Their attacks toppled New York City's famous World Trade Center, killing thousands. Both events, he said, were so unreal, so improbable that they felt like things plucked from a novelist's head. He has often called moments like these to be so strange and so unlikely that they can be beautiful to a novelist.

Japan's 9/11

A 2011 tsunami, triggered by an earthquake, caused massive damage in Japan, including to a nuclear power plant.

But the Japanese people lost so much in the disaster that Murakami said it forced the country and everyone living in it to change the way they think about what is important. Maybe it's not about fancy cars or technology or about how much money you can save in a bank, he said. Now people were focusing more on freedom and time spent doing things they enjoyed with the people they love.

New Priorities

Freedom and time, he said, were the most important things anyone can have. While not very comfortable giving speeches, people looked to Murakami as the voice of Japan during this disaster, and he responded by speaking out against the government for not ensuring that nuclear power plants could withstand an earthquake. He spoke in gentle terms, giving people what they needed most: hope. This speech was one of the rare times that Murakami made his political feelings known and went outside of his comfort zone.

During a speech he gave in Barcelona after winning an award, Murakami addressed the crisis:

> The recent earthquake came as a tremendous shock for almost all Japanese. Even we Japanese who are so accustomed to earthquakes were completely overwhelmed by the sheer scale of the damage. Gripped by a sense of powerlessness, we feel uncertainty about the future of our country. But, in time, we will pull ourselves together mentally and devote ourselves to the task of reconstruction. I am not that concerned about that point. We are a nation

9/11

Japan's disaster has been compared in scope to the terrorist attacks on the United States that occurred on September 11, 2001—now known as 9/11. Japan's disaster was an act of nature, while 9/11 was an act of war.

It was during the morning of September 11 that Muslim extremists acting on the orders of Osama bin Laden hijacked four planes in the United States with the plan of simultaneously crashing them into high-profile and highly-populated areas.

Two planes were flown into the "Twin Towers," which were the tallest skyscrapers in New York and the main buildings of the World Trade Center. The buildings collapsed shortly after they were struck, and roughly 3,000 people were killed.

A third plane crashed into the Pentagon in Washington, D.C., killing many. The hijackers aboard the fourth plane were trying to fly it into the White House when passengers aboard the plane learned of the other three planes and wrestled control of the aircraft from the terrorists. The plane crashed in a field in Pennsylvania killing all aboard the plane, but saving the White House from damage.

The attacks prompted the United States to wage the "War on Terror" that has lasted many years and has sent American troops to Iraq and Afghanistan. Osama bin Laden was eventually hunted down by American troops and was shot and killed.

Today, 9/11 or September 11, is a day of reflection and remembrance honoring those who lost their lives.

that has survived a long history of such disasters. We will not continue to be stunned by the blow forever. The damaged homes will be rebuilt and the damaged roads will be repaired.

Ultimately, we have appropriated this planet called earth for ourselves. It's not as if the earth came up and asked us, "Please come live here." Just because the ground shakes a bit is not a reason to complain. After all, such is the nature of the earth that it shakes from time to time. We have no choice but to live together with nature, whether we like it or not.[3]

While he was very critical of the Japanese government for allowing the nuclear disaster, the tsunami, earthquake, and nuclear meltdown were the basis for one of his most anticipated novels: *Colourless Tsukuru Tazaki and His Years of Pilgrimage*. Like many of his previous novels, the book centers around a main character who is lonely and spends a lot of time looking back over his life. He reflects on missed opportunities and the things he could have done differently. This time he has to deal with the feelings of loss that everyone seemed to suffer after the disaster.

And even though he had planned to write a story that dealt with the earthquake and tsunami, it's no surprise that he wasn't quite sure where the story would lead him. "One day I just felt like it, and I sat at my desk and started to write the first few lines of this story," he said. "Then for about half a year, I continued to write this story without knowing anything like what would happen, what type of people would appear and how long the story would be."[4]

Japan's 9/11

Murakami was photographed in 2013 upon his arrival in Kyoto to speak about *Colorless Tsukuru Tazaki and His Years of Pilgrimage.*

Murakami groups the sarin gas attack, the Kobe earthquake, and the 2010 tsunami and nuclear meltdown among the four worst disasters in Japanese history. The other? The two atomic bombs dropped on Japan by the United States during the final days of World War II that killed thousands and destroyed cities.

Chapter 10

A Future Nobel Prize?

The highest honor for a novelist—other than people reading and loving your books—is to be awarded the Nobel Prize for Literature. And, even though Haruki Murakami is as popular around the world as he is in his native Japan, he has yet to win the award. Still, most critics and fans agree that one day he will win that honor.

In fact, every fall, there are websites touting and articles detailing the odds for Murakami to win the award. People even make bets whether this will be the year he wins the prize. And while he appreciates the enthusiasm of his fans and supporters, Murakami does not like being constantly asked about his odds to finally win the award.

No Interest in Awards

He has actually called it annoying and reminds his fans that this is not a horse race. For Murakami, awards are secondary to his main goal of offering readers a diversion. He has often mentioned that the average Japanese office worker spends more than two hours a day traveling to and from work on the trains. He wants to offer them a diversion, a page-turning book they can immerse themselves in while commuting—an escape from the everyday tasks that await them at work. He would rather remain popular than win awards.

Still, the Nobel Prize for Literature can represent a sense of pride for a nation and is taken very seriously in Japan, where pride and honor took on even greater meaning after the reconstruction of the country after World War II. Japan rose from the rubble of destruction to once again become an economic world power.

Only two Japanese authors—Kenzaburo Oe and Yasunari Kawabata—have ever won the acclaimed award. Japan has also been awarded a few Nobel Prizes in the field of physics. Murakami has been awarded every single literary prize that Japan offers, including the prestigious Yomiuri Literary Prize.

Only One Thing Matters

Like most successful writers, Murakami insists that he never thinks about winning the Nobel Prize or any award for that matter. Only one thing matters to him as a novelist. "The most valuable thing of all are

A Future Nobel Prize?

The Nobel Prize for Literature

The Nobel Prize for Literature was first given out in the year 1901, and it is awarded every year to an author for the most outstanding work throughout their careers.

The award was established by Alfred Nobel in his will, and the winners are chosen by the Swedish Academy. Nobel's will also decreed four other annual Nobel Prizes. They are in the fields of chemistry, physics, physiology or medicine, and the Nobel Peace Prize, which is awarded by the Norwegian Nobel Committee to the individual that does the most to promote peace and brotherhood among different countries.

Due to a discrepancy in how the rules were originally interpreted, many great writers like Anton Chekhov, Leo Tolstoy, and James Joyce were never awarded the prize.

Roughly 200 nominations are made annually, and the committee narrows the list down to five finalists. They then spend the next several months reading all the work before deciding on the winner. The nominations and short lists are kept secret for fifty years. The winner receives a gold medal, a citation and diploma, and a fluctuating sum of money.

Some of the winners, like Jean-Paul Sartre, have refused to accept the award, saying they do not write in order to win awards. Some of the great American writers who have garnered the award include Ernest Hemingway, John Steinbeck, and Eugene O'Neill. The most recent American winner was Toni Morrison, author of *The Bluest Eye* and *Beloved*, among others.

good readers," he said. "Whatever prize, decoration, or favorable review I get, compared to the people who use their own money to go out and buy my books, [the prizes] hold no meaning."[1] One might say that a writer or novelist must first write for themselves and be true to their craft before their work can appeal to others.

So where do those quirky characters and unique and strange ideas come from? It's simple. Murakami has said that he simply looks deep down within himself for the words that wind up on paper in the hands of his fans. "I'm looking for my own story. I'm digging the surface and descending to my own soul," he said, adding that he hopes his books offer his readers "a sense of freedom—freedom from the real world."[2]

Treasure Chest

And as he gets older, Murakami continues to reach deep within himself to find the dark, fantastic stories that offer escape and freedom from the real world. And he hopes to keep doing it for as long as there are stories in his head.

But, as he explained, he continuously tries to store memories and ideas in an imaginary treasure chest in his mind that has been filled with alternate realities, little people, talking cats, fish falling from the sky, and magical pinball machines. "I have collected so many memories, in my chest, the chest of my mind," he said. "I think everybody has a lot of memories of his or her own, but it's a special gift to find the right drawer. I can do that. If I need something, I can point to the right drawer."[3]

A Future Nobel Prize?

Kenzaburo Oe is one of only two Japanese writers to win the Nobel Prize in Literature.

Maybe his brain remains so fertile and rich with stories because he often spends time translating English novels into Japanese for his fellow countrymen to read and writes nonfiction every once in a while. These activities expose him to other cultures, other ideas, and other styles of writing.

In 2009, Murakami published what many feel to be a masterpiece, the massive 928-page *1Q84*, which he spent four years writing. The book was released in Japan over two years as a three-volume set and deals with alternate histories, a parallel universe, and a main character who in her haste to get to a meeting, opens a door and winds up in a different but similar reality.

The first print run sold out the very first day it was available.

The book, and especially the title, is an homage, or tribute, to one of Murakami's favorite authors, George Orwell, whose most well-known books include *Animal Farm* and *1984*.

The letter "Q" in Japanese is pronounced "nine," so the title of Murakami's classic is pronounced 1984. Murakami said that Orwell's classic was written about the near-future, while his book looks back at the same year and is about the near-past.

Murakami reread the Orwell book while writing *1Q84* to help keep his own ideas fresh. He also wanted to make sure he was writing pure fiction. Orwell, who was also a journalist, often disguised his political feelings or criticisms in his fiction. That was something Murakami

A Future Nobel Prize?

wanted to avoid. "I guess (Orwell and I) have a common feeling against the system," Murakami said. "George Orwell is half journalist, half fiction writer. I'm 100 percent fiction writer. I don't want to write messages. I want to write good stories."[4]

George Orwell's writings, particularly *1984*, influenced Haruki Murakami. Murakami's *1Q84* was written as an homage to the British novelist's mid-twentieth century dystopian novel.

Orwell's *1984*

Eric Arthur Blair was born in England in 1903. The world would know him by his pen name, or writing name, George Orwell. He was a journalist and author whose work was marked by his strong feelings against social injustice and dictatorship governments. His two most well-known works are *Animal Farm* and the futuristic novel *1984*, which he wrote in 1949.

The novel *1984* is set in a scary, undesirable future. The book spawned the phrase, "Big Brother is watching." Big Brother is the tyrannical government leader of this fictional society where the government secretly watches people to make sure they are doing what they are told. Orwell originally called the book *The Last Man in Europe*, before changing it.

The main character in the book is named Winston Smith. His job for the government is to continuously change historical documents so that future generations believe everything the government tells them. But in doing his job, Winston becomes curious about the true past and real history. He finds a spot near one of Big Brother's cameras where he cannot be seen. There he begins writing a secret journal in which he criticizes the government. If he is caught, Winston will surely be executed.

The book became an almost instant classic even though critics described it as frightening and depressing. The book was so influential that the term *Orwellian* is used today to describe surreal and undesirable cultures or views of the future.

A Future Nobel Prize?

Dreaming While Awake

The stories are not only good but they have also transformed Japanese literature—and literature in general—with unforgettable characters and unpredictable scenarios. But no matter how much fame Murakami achieves in his life, he has never forgotten how it all started.

Murakami has always remembered and held close to his heart the magical lore of wandering around a bookstore and the wonderful memories it created. That was one of the reasons why in August 2015, the author decided to write an essay about his life as a novelist and *not* make it available to online booksellers like Amazon. It was sold only in bookstores. The idea behind the move was to force people away from their computers and into an actual bookstore.

The book, *Novelist as an Profession*, was released in September in Japan and became a best-selling book, showing how hungry readers are for anything by Murakami. So, just how long does Murakami intend to keep writing? "I don't know what's going to happen," he said. "I have no idea—when I am 80 years old, what will I write? I don't know. Maybe I'm running and writing. That would be great. But nobody knows."[5]

The man who grew up loving jazz and Western literature and never quite seemed to fit the image his parents wanted for him, eventually chose novelist as his occupation, and the world is a better place for it. Much

Haruki Murakami: Best-Selling Author

Regardless of the prizes he wins and the acclaim Murakami receives, his writing has earned him place on our literary landscape.

to the delight of millions around the world, Murakami is a man who puts his waking dreams to paper.

And thank goodness for that. "The good thing about writing books is that you can dream while you are awake," he said. "If it's a real dream, you cannot control it."[6]

Chronology

1945—The United States drops two atom bombs on Japan, ending World War II.

1949—Haruki Murakami is born in Kyoto, Japan.

1961—Murakami reads his first English novel.

1964—Murakami attends his first jazz concert and is hooked.

1969—Murakami gets married against his parents' wishes.

1974—Murakami and his wife open a jazz club called the Peter Cat.

1978—Murakami attends a baseball game and decides to become an author.

1979—His first book, *Hear the Wind Sing*, is awarded a major prize by a Japanese magazine.

1980—Murakami writes his second book, *Pinball*.

1982—The third book in the "Trilogy of the Rat," *A Wild Sheep Chase*, is published.

1987—Murakami writes the instant classic *Norwegian Wood*.

1991—Murakami attends a fellowship in the United States where he works as a professor at Princeton University.

1995—Murakami is awarded the prestigious Yomiuri Literary Prize.

CHRONOLOGY

1994—The *Wind-Up Bird Chronicle* is published.

1995—Terrorists attack the Tokyo subways with poison gas.

1996—Murakami runs his first ultramarathon.

1997—Murakami writes his first nonfiction account of the poison gas attacks entitled *Underground*.

2002—Murakami writes *Kafka on the Shore*.

2006—Murakami becomes the sixth recipient of the Kafka Literary Prize.

2009–2010—Murakami writes the three-volume book *1Q84*.

2011—A massive earthquake strikes Japan causing a tsunami and nuclear meltdown.

2013—Murakami's novel, *Colorless Tsukuru Tazaki and His Years of Pilgrimage*, is published and sells out instantly in many countries.

2015—Murakami writes *Novelist as a Profession*.

Chapter Notes

Chapter 1. Only One of Six

1. Haruki Murakami, http://www.harukimurakami.com/q_and_a/a-conversation-with-haruki-murakami-about-sputnik-sweetheart (retrieved Oct. 9, 2015).

2. Ibid.

3. Ibid.

4. Ibid.

5. Howard W. French, "Seeing a Clash of Social Networks; A Japanese Writer Analyzes Terrorists and Their Victims," *New York Times*, Oct. 15, 2001, http://www.nytimes.com/2001/10/15/arts/seeing-clash-social-networks-japanese-writer-analyzes-terrorists-their-victims.html.

Chapter 2. Destiny

1. "Japan's Emperor: A Mortal Man," *New York Times*, Jan. 7, 1989, http://www.nytimes.com/1989/01/07/opinion/japan-s-emperor-a-mortal-man.html (retrieved Oct. 13, 2015).

2. Cool Japan Illustrated, "Murakami, Haruki," http://www.cool-jp.com/articles/haruki/haruki_fs_parent.php?article_id=115&parent_category_id=8 (retrieved Oct. 13, 2015).

3. Ibid.

Chapter 3. Rebelling

1. Sam Anderson, "The Fierce Imagination of Haruki Marakumi," *New York Times*, Oct. 21, 2011, http://www.nytimes.com/2011/10/23/magazine/

CHAPTER NOTES

the-fierce-imagination-of-haruki-murakami.
html?pagewanted=all&_r=1 (retrieved Oct. 14, 2015).

2. Cool Japan Illustrated, "Murakami, Haruki," http://www.cool-jp.com/articles/haruki/haruki_fs_parent.php?article_id=115&parent_category_id=8 (retrieved Oct. 13, 2015).

3. Ibid.

Chapter 4. Western Influence

1. Matt Thompson, "Nobel Prize Winner in Waiting?" *The Guardian Newspaper*, May 26, 2001, http://www.theguardian.com/books/2001/may/26/fiction.harukimurakami (retrieved Oct. 20, 2015).

2. "Haruki Murakami's Passion for Jazz," *Open Culture*, http://www.openculture.com/2014/07/haruki-murakamis-passion-for-jazz.html (retrieved Oct. 20, 2015).

Chapter 5. Finding His Way

1. Emma Brockes, "Haruki Murakami: I Took a Gamble and Survived," *The Guardian Newspaper*, Oct. 14, 2011, http://www.theguardian.com/books/2011/oct/14/haruki-murakami-1q84 (retrieved Oct. 22, 2015).

2. Ibid.

3. Ibid.

4. Matt Thompson, "Nobel Prize Winner in Waiting?" *The Guardian Newspaper*, May 26, 2001, http://www.theguardian.com/books/2001/may/26/fiction.harukimurakami (retrieved Oct. 20, 2015).

Chapter 6. Baseball

1. Haruki Murakami, *Wind/Pinball: Two Novels* (New York: Alfred A. Knopf Publishers, trans., 2015), p. 4.

2. Bradley Campbell, "A Baseball Player Hits a Double and It Launches the Career of Haruki Murakami," *Public Radio International,* Sept. 3, 2015, http://www.pri.org/stories/2015-09-03/baseball-player-hits-double-and-it-launches-career-haruki-murakami (retrieved Oct. 27, 2015).

Chapter 7. Best-Selling Author

1. Haruki Murakami, *Wind/Pinball: Two Novels* (New York: Alfred A. Knopf Publishers, trans., 2015), p. 6.

2. Ibid.

3. Sam Anderson, "The Fierce Imagination of Haruki Marakumi," *New York Times*, Oct. 21, 2011, http://www.nytimes.com/2011/10/23/magazine/the-fierce-imagination-of-haruki-murakami.html?pagewanted=all&_r=1 (retrieved Oct. 14, 2015).

4. Emma Brockes, "Haruki Murakami: I Took a Gamble and Survived," *The Guardian Newspaper*, Oct. 14, 2011, http://www.theguardian.com/books/2011/oct/14/haruki-murakami-1q84 (retrieved Oct. 22, 2015).

Chapter 8. Running to Commercial Success

1. Sam Anderson, "The Fierce Imagination of Haruki Marakumi," *New York Times*, Oct. 21, 2011, http://www.nytimes.com/2011/10/23/magazine/the-fierce-imagination-of-haruki-murakami.html?pagewanted=all&_r=1 (retrieved Oct. 14, 2015).

2. *Spiegel Magazine* online, "When I Run I Am in a Peaceful Place," Feb. 20, 2008, http://www.spiegel.de/international/world/spiegel-interview-with-haruki-murakami-when-i-run-i-am-in-a-peaceful-place-a-536608.html (retrieved Nov. 5, 2015).

3. Ibid.

4. Ibid.

CHAPTER 9. JAPAN'S 9/11

1. Matt Thompson, "Nobel Prize Winner in Waiting?" *The Guardian Newspaper,* May 26, 2001, http://www.theguardian.com/books/2001/may/26/fiction.harukimurakami (retrieved Oct. 20, 2015).

2. Emma Brockes, "Haruki Murakami: I Took a Gamble and Survived," *The Guardian Newspaper,* Oct. 14, 2011, http://www.theguardian.com/books/2011/oct/14/haruki-murakami-1q84 (retrieved Oct. 22, 2015).

3. Speech by Murakami Haruki on the Occasion of Receiving the International Catalunya Prize, June 9, 2011, http://japanfocus.org/-Murakami-Haruki/3571/article.html (retrieved Nov. 10, 2015).

4. Justin McCurry and Alison Floyd, "Haruki Murakami Fans Que Overnight for His Latest Novel," *The Guardian Newspaper,* April 12, 2013, http://www.theguardian.com/books/2013/apr/12/haruki-murakami-colourless-tsukuru-tazaki (retrieved Nov. 10, 2015).

Chapter 10. A Future Nobel Prize?

1. Audrey Akcasu, "Nobel Prize for Literature Eludes Japan's Haruki Murakami Yet Again and He Couldn't Care Less," *Rocket News* 24, Oct. 12, 2015, http://en.rocketnews24.com/2015/10/12/nobel-prize-for-literature-eludes-japans-haruki-murakami-yet-again-and-he-couldnt-care-less/ (retrieved Nov. 13, 2015).

2. Matt Thompson, "Nobel Prize Winner in Waiting?" *The Guardian Newspaper*, May 26, 2001, http://www.theguardian.com/books/2001/may/26/fiction.harukimurakami (retrieved Oct. 20, 2015).

3. Steven Poole, "Haruki Murakami: I'm an Outcast in the Japanese Literary World," *The Guardian Newspaper*, Sept. 13, 2014, http://www.theguardian.com/books/2014/sep/13/haruki-murakami-interview-colorless-tsukur-tazaki-and-his-years-of-pilgrimage (retrieved Nov. 14, 2015).

4. Sam Anderson, "The Fierce Imagination of Haruki Marakumi," *New York Times*, Oct. 21, 2011, http://www.nytimes.com/2011/10/23/magazine/the-fierce-imagination-of-haruki-murakami.html?pagewanted=all&_r=1 (retrieved Oct. 14, 2015).

5. Poole.

6. John Wray, "Haruki Murakami, The Art of Fiction No. 182," *The Paris Review*, Sept. 2004, http://www.theparisreview.org/interviews/2/the-art-of-fiction-no-182-haruki-murakami (retrieved Nov. 14, 2015).

Glossary

critical—Being of the utmost importance or expressing disapproving comments.

crystallizing—When something forms and takes a definite shape.

devastation—To overwhelmingly destroy something.

dialogue—Conversation between people or the lines spoken by characters in a book.

extortion—Obtaining money in an illegal manner by using threats or power.

fertile—Something that is rich in material, whether crops or good ideas.

hailed—Praising someone or their deeds in a tribute.

horrific—Something that causes terror and fear.

immortal—A person or being that lives forever and cannot die.

isolate—To keep an object or person away from everything else.

memoir—A person's life story in their own words.

metropolis—A big city or urban area that is considered the center of activity.

militaristic—A society in which the armed forces rule the government.

symmetrical—Being similar in shape and size.

tactile—Something that relates to having a sense of touch.

Further Reading

Books

Curry, Mason. *Daily Rituals: How Artists Work.* New York: Alfred A. Knopf, 2013.

Murakami, Haruki. *Norwegian Wood.* New York: Vintage International, 2000.

Murakami, Haruki. *What I Talk About When I Talk About Running.* New York: Alfred A. Knopf, 2008.

Stretcher, Carl Matthew. *The Forbidden Worlds of Haruki Murakami.* Minneapolis: University of Minnesota Press, 2014.

Websites

Haruki Murakami
Huarukimurakami.com
Official website of the renowned author

Famous Authors
www.famousauthors.org/haruki-murakami
Online resource about Haruki Murakami

The Japan Times
www.japantimes.co.jp/tag/haruki-murakami/
Online versions of articles written about author Haruki Murakami

Index

A
After the Quake, 96
atomic bomb, 7, 8, 22, 23, 25, 104
Aum Shinrikyo, 9, 10, 15, 16

B
Buddhism, 21, 22
Bushido, 18

C
Catcher in the Rye, The, 41, 84, 86
Chandler, Raymond, 40–44
Colorless Tsukuru Tazaki and His Years of Pilgrimage, 102–103
crystallizing moment 65–66

D
Davis, Miles, 47, 49
democracy, 25

E
earthquakes. *See* Japan
Emperor Hirohito, 20

F
Fukushima, 97

G
Great Depression, 17
Gunzo, 73–74, 76

H
Hear the Wind Sing, 65, 68, 74, 76
Hemingway, Ernest, 72, 74–75, 107
Hilton, Dave, 63, 65

J
Japan
  baseball, 62
  culture, 12–13, 18, 21–22, 27–28, 36, 44
  earthquake (1995), 96
  earthquake (2011), 97–104
  literature, 24, 26, 37–39, 44
  occupation, 24–25, 27
jazz, 45, 47–49, 53, 55–56, 58–59, 65–66, 73, 76, 78, 80, 113

K
Kawabata, Yasunari, 44, 106
Kobe, 30–33, 45, 94, 96, 104
Kristof, Agota, 70
Kyoto, 21, 22, 24, 30, 103

L

Lost Generation, 75

M

MacArthur, Douglas A., 25
magical realism, 76, 79, 81–83
Mahjong, 47
marathons, 89–92
Marlowe, Phillip, 41, 43
Marquez, Gabriel Garcia, 79, 81
Murakami, Chiaki (father), 17, 21–22, 24, 28, 30, 32, 36, 56, 54
Murakami, Haruki,
  awards and honors, 80, 105–115
  baseball, 61–65
  childhood, 29–34
  education, 32–39, 45, 49–51, 53–55
  health, 87–89
  family, 17, 22, 80
  jazz club, 56–59
  routine, 78–80
  running, 89–93
  sarin gas attacks, 10, 12–15
  success, 83–93, 113–114
  Western influence, 27–28, 32, 40–50
  writing in English, 68–71
Murakami, Mansori, 61
Murakami, Mikuyi (mother), 17, 21, 24, 27, 30
Murakami, Yoko (wife), 55–56, 58–59, 66, 74, 78, 80, 98

N

9/11, 89, 101
1984, 110–112
Nobel Prize, 44, 75, 105–107
Norwegian Wood, 84–85
Novelist as a Profession, 113

O

Oe, Kenxaburo, 106, 109
1Q84, 110–111
Orwell, George, 110–112
Osaka, 21, 33

P

Peter Cat, The, 59, 76, 78
Pinball, 76, 78
Presley, Elvis, 44, 46

R

rock-and-roll music, 44–45, 48, 84

S

Salinger, J. D., 41, 86
sarin gas, 7, 9–10, 14, 16, 95, 104
Shinto, 35

INDEX

T

Tale of Heike, The, 24
themes, 13, 15, 24 ,27, 32,
   35, 37, 68, 79, 80, 96
   nostalgia, 32
   water, 29–30
Tokyo, 7, 8, 10, 14, 25, 53,
   56, 57, 63, 88, 95

U

Underground, 12, 13, 15, 95
   "Blind Nightmare, Where
      Are We Japanese
      Going?" 15

W

Waseda University, 53
*What I Talk About When I
   Talk About Running*,
   91–92
Wild Sheep Chase, A, 80, 81
*Wind Up Bird Chronicle,
   The,* 30
World War I, 17
World War II, 7, 8, 18,
   22–25, 27, 33, 44, 57,
   1004, 106

Y

Yakult Swallows, 63–64
Yomiuri Literary Prize, 106